The Secret Path of Ned the Ninja

Book One
Reluctant Hero

Melissa Mertz
Kea Alwang

The Secret Path of Ned the Ninja: Reluctant Hero is a work of fiction. Names, characters, places, and incidents are the products of the authors' imaginations or are used fictitiously.

ISBN-13: 978-1496133311
ISBN-10: 1496133315

Library of Congress Control Number: 2014904543

Rounded Star Media, LLC
Paramus, New Jersey
Printed in the United States of America

Contact the authors at:
mail@nedtheninja.com
kea@keaalwang.com
www.nedtheninja.com
www.keaalwang.com

Cover Illustration: C. Spliedt
www.runrabbitproductions.com

Dedicated to:

Tiger Jack ...
my peace on Earth

William & Sylvia Alwang ...
for more than I can write

Our greatest glory is not in never falling,
but in rising every time we fall.

- Confucius

ACKNOWLEDGMENTS

The authors thank their Isshin-Ryu Family Tree for inspiration in teaching "the silent way" and for being superior examples of mind over matter:

Tatsuo Shimabuku
the founder of Isshin-Ryu karate

Grand Master Richard Mrofka (The Siberian Tiger)
10th-Degree Black Belt in Isshin-Ryu karate
Founder of the *Tiger Commando Fighting System*

Professor Ronald Allen Mertz
9th-Degree Black Belt in Isshin-Ryu karate
Master Melissa Mertz's sensei and father
"All little girls think their fathers are the heroes of the world. My perception of my Dad is no different." --MM

Master Franco Musano
6th-Degree Black Belt Master in Isshin-Ryu Karate
Master Melissa Mertz's training partner
Honored Teacher at *The Dojo Paramus*

A huge thank you to the students of *The Dojo Paramus* in New Jersey who, for over ten years, have been the most amazing group of kids to teach.

Cool Beans Cafe in Oradell, New Jersey: Thank you for energy via your delicious coffees and teas and for providing a super-cool, relaxing atmosphere in which to work.

Mr. Bill Kane, a man who exemplifies what it means to live in the moment and who radiates positive energy to all around. We credit him with being the calming, intellectual presence in the lobby of *The Dojo Paramus.*

CHAPTER ONE

I knew it was coming. It was only a matter of time, really. Mom and Dad had wanted me to take karate lessons for two years, but I always refused. Truth is, I'm more of a liberal arts kind of guy. I read a lot, write a lot ... get swindled out of my lunch money a lot. Hey, I would complain, but my school's cafeteria food makes me wonder if starving for a day is really such a bad thing. If I think about it, getting shaken down for $3.50 actually pays for itself by saving my weak stomach from Mystery Meat Mondays.

By now, you've probably decided I'm not the most confrontational kind of guy. If so, you've hit the nerd on the head. I don't mean to brag, but I'll walk the long way around my block to the corner mailbox just to avoid the *possibility* of my arch nemesis, Beck the Bonebreaker, seeing me walk past his house. (We call that strategy, folks.) And guess who lines up last on the school lunch line to avoid trouble when Beck the Bonebreaker decides to push his way to the front? Ever have your most powerful *Legendary Pokemon* card stolen? Did you get it back? Well, I may have spent fifty dollars of my birthday money buying new card packs until I found that card again, but at least I didn't spend 50 days in the hospital courtesy of—you guessed it—Beck the Bonebreaker.

Batman had the Joker. Superman had Lex Luthor. Harry Potter had Voldemort. I have Jared Beck. And Jared Beck is the biggest fifth grader you've ever seen. He's also scary ugly, which I know sounds mean. But when you're always snarling, scowling, and pushing people around, how can you look anything *but* ugly? (And I mean *butt* ugly.) One kid named Bill Huber—rest in peace, man—started a rumor last year, just before school ended, that Beck is half yeti. Officially, we heard Bill moved unexpectedly over the summer. I'm not so sure. Still, nobody has dared to call Beck anything close to a bigfoot-type beast again.

If you think *that's* scary, try this: Beck named *himself* Beck the Bonebreaker after he pushed Angel Martino off a bike. Once we all saw Martino with his arm in a cast, nobody dared question it. If you want the truth, I'm just surprised it wasn't me who wound up in a cast.

Now that you know how Jared Beck got his nickname, I suppose it doesn't take much imagination (and Beck has none) to believe Beck dubbed me, Ned the Nerd.

Anyway, my Mom and Dad are the type of parents who trust me to make my own decisions. But today they took matters into their own hands and turned a sunny day in April into doomsday. Why the change in parenting style? Well, I came home from school with (count 'em) two rope-burned hands, one bruised jaw, one bump on the back of the head, two bruised hips, and a mean paper cut. Now before you get to thinking Beck the Bonebreaker managed to inflict all that pain, I can only give him credit for the bruised hips and the hill growing out of my head. Apparently, my hips had a tough time squeezing into the locker he stuffed me into, but my head went in rather smoothly before hitting the wall behind it. The burns on my hands came from climbing the knotted rope in gym—and rather quickly sliding down as my biceps demanded to know who I thought I was kidding. Likewise, I only have myself to blame for slamming my jaw on the ground after tripping over an untied shoe lace. (Okay, so I was running away from Beck's best friend Richie Kaufman, but at least he wasn't Beck.) Finally, my Spanish textbook gave me the paper cut. (*Ay! Caramba!*) Did I mention I'm lucky I can put one foot in front of the other?

Trouble was, Mom and Dad wouldn't accept the explanations for my injuries this time. They thought I made up the rope, the shoe lace, and the textbook. They blamed Beck the Bonebreaker for all of my injuries and themselves for not teaching me to stick up for myself.

"Mom," I said, "How could Beck have given me a paper cut?"

"He took your lunch money again, didn't he? Just ripped that five-dollar bill straight out of your hand, am I right? I know I'm right."

My Mom should've been a writer. She can throw around plots, twists, and conspiracy theories like nobody's business!

"No, Mom. I ate today." Then I opened my eyes real wide, slammed my hand on the kitchen table and said, "Hey, I've got it! Maybe my Spanish book is working for Beck. Yeah, that's it. Maybe tomorrow it will slam my fingers between its covers."

Dad chimed in: "Don't get wise with your mother, Mister."

But Mom was already working on pulling her thoughts together. And that's always fun to watch. "Well ... I ... your father and I feel ... we ... enough is enough ... that boy ... you can't ... matters ... hands ... own ... the dog!"

Poor Cracker Jack whined the confused sound canines make when they wonder what they did this time. He tracked Mom with his hound dog eyes, droopy lids twitching, wondering if he should make a break for the living room.

Personally, I love when Mom gets flustered and frazzled;

she turns into a blithering cartoon character. Don't get me wrong—I love my mom. It's just that my inability to think on my feet came from somewhere, so if I didn't laugh over it, I think I would cry.

Today, however, was no ordinary day. Without warning, my frazzled mother suddenly looked me straight in the eyes, hands on hips, completely in control of her thoughts in a way I hadn't witnessed before. No, she suddenly became very UN-frazzled. And, she was done blithering.

I froze. Terror set in. Cracker Jack got up, tail down, and slinked out of the kitchen. He didn't know what that look meant, but he didn't like it. I, however, had a frightening little suspicion over what had happened. It was as if some emergency parenting app in Mom's brain fired up and kicked into gear. Slowly, her expression became more intense than the time she forced my teacher to offer me an extra-credit assignment so that I wouldn't fail gym again. Apparently, when Mom decided her little Nedsy's future was looking dark, she became the very thing most kids find more embarrassing than puking on the school bus. She became ... a mom on a mission.

DARN YOU, JARED BECK!

"You," Mom hissed, then paused long enough for me to fall to my knees and start pleading, "will start karate this very week ... even if your father and I have to drag you there."

CHAPTER TWO

After the last of my fingers lost their grip on the door frame of *Tora Khan Martial Arts*, I stumbled into a lobby full of kids in blue outfits. And they were armed with sticks— big sticks. I suppose you have to carry something like that if you're going to walk around in baggy pants and a bathrobe all day. I mean if I were going to fight—which I wasn't—I would want to wear something a bit more streamlined. You know, like a super-thin, ultra-shock-absorbing, invisibility-capable, polypropinetic suit of armor. Okay, you've got me. I made that one up. (The word *polypropinetic*, doesn't exist, so don't bother looking it up.) But doesn't that sound like the world's best superhero costume? Notice I left out the cape. Capes are lame.

So I stood there, armed with nothing but my wit, when, to my left, a shout thundered into the lobby. I jumped backward into my dad, then leaned forward to peek through a doorway. There, in a large room with a blue floor, stood a woman in black pants and a white bathrobe, hands on hips. As she stared down at a kid in blue who had fallen flat onto his back, she smiled. Not only did she not see a problem with throwing a kid to the floor like a sack of dirty laundry, she clearly enjoyed it. Why would they put such a big student in with kids my age? Where was the karate teacher? Would he make her do a million pushups as punishment? I mean, what did that kid to do her?

Mom began inching me toward the doorway by pressing her knuckles into my spine.

"Quit it!" I whispered through my teeth. "Why don't you take me to Alcatraz, put me in a dress and send me into the prison yard while you're at it."

"Don't be silly, Sweetie. That prison closed years ago."

"I'm thinking they reopened it here!"

"*Aswate!*" the woman's voice boomed through the doorway. Ten kids suddenly dropped to their knees.

"As-what-did-she-say?" I asked Dad.

Dad shrugged.

"Ray!" the woman boomed again.

I leaned into the classroom to see which of the kids, clearly in trouble, was Ray. But all ten students suddenly put their heads to the ground. They couldn't all be Ray, but one thing was certain: None of them wanted to see what would happen to the poor guy.

Then it dawned on me. 'Super Girl' was the karate teacher. The next time Beck tells me I fight like a girl, he could be right.

The students suddenly formed a moving line, each one bowing to the karate teacher before exiting the classroom and entering the lobby. They sure did a lot of bowing around here. Wonderful. As if life hasn't got me bowing down enough?

Finally, the teacher came out to the lobby—and headed straight for me. I'd like to say I jumped into some fancy karate pose, ready to defend myself, but the truth was ... I hid behind Dad.

"You must be Ned!" the teacher said cheerfully. I stepped away from Dad and noticed her smile was real nice—not at all scary. But then she pulled an elastic band out of her dark ponytail, shook out her hair, and tied it back again so fast that I wondered if she meant to distract me. I nailed my feet to the floor. Nobody was throwing me to the ground without a fight—or at least a few strong words. After all, I needed these chicken legs of mine for running away from Beck.

"I'm Sensei Melissa," she said, shook hands with my parents, then offered her hand to me.

I decided to risk taking it. My theory? If I wound up in the hospital, then I couldn't come to karate class, now could I? What do they say about an ounce of prevention and a pound of cure?

The teacher shook my hand and smiled again.

11

I smiled back, simply because I was still on my feet. Although, in my head, I was pretty much floored. So far, nothing here was anything I expected.

"So are you ready to try karate today, Ned?" asked the teacher.

Here was my chance. "Actually, no. Not really. Not today," I sputtered.

Dad's hand slammed down on my shoulder. "That's our Ned! Always the kidder. Truthfully, all he's been talking about is coming to karate today."

That's my Dad. Lying through his teeth without actually lying. Yes, I had been talking about karate all morning and every minute the night before. I said things like, "Not doing it! No way, no how!" and, "Do I get to pick out my wheelchair when every bone in my body is broken? I'd like a red one. But for my casket ... and this is important ... I would like your apology to me etched into the lid." Then, just before we left the house, I said, "Mom, are you really going to let your wittle, wittle, baby boy get karate chopped into a million pieces?"

Want to know what she said? My mother—the one who brought me into this world and didn't let me eat anything bigger than a chocolate chip until I was four years old so that I wouldn't choke? The one who sat up with me all night when I had the flu? The one who bought me ice cream when I flunked gym class? The one who thought tag was too dangerous a game? *That* mother? She looked me straight in the eye and said, "You'll live."

"Thank you, Sensei! See you next week," shouted a cheerful kid on his way out the door. It was the poor sucker who got thrown to the floor. Man, he looked happy.

The teacher waved. "See you Thursday, Christopher! Nice back hands today."

"Are we going to do take-downs again on Thursday?" the boy asked.

"You bet."

"Yes!" The kid pumped his fist in the air and practically danced out of the building.

That did it.

"Dad, can I speak with you a moment?"

Dad looked embarrassed, then smiled at the teacher and said, "Excuse us one moment, please."

I pulled Dad aside by the arm and gritted my teeth so that nobody could read my lips. "Don't you sense something wrong here, Dad?"

"Like what? Other than you being very rude, of course."

"There's mind control going on here. That kid *wants* to be flipped to the floor again!"

"Maybe it's fun, Ned. Did you ever think of that?"

"Okay, if that's fun, then I'll just go up to Beck each day, call him a girlie-man, then get thrown to the ground for free. You don't have to pay karate tuition, Dad. Deal? Put the money in my college fund. If you make me do this, I might not be alive long enough to use it."

Dad said nothing as he led me back to the teacher. "Ned's all yours, Sensei Melissa."

"Come on, Ned. Next class starts in five minutes. I'll show you where to put your shoes and socks."

I had noticed that a few kids wore their socks in the matted room. "Um, do I have to take off my socks?"

"No, you may leave them on. But it's easier to slip on the mats with socks. The rule here is clean feet or clean socks—your choice."

Eureka! I knew what could get me kicked out of karate: The night before my next class, I would create the stinkiest, most unclean feet that ever stepped onto those mats. I would run around the backyard with three layers of used gym socks on my feet, then sleep with the socks on. But not before stuffing them with pieces of Gouda, cheddar, and Gorgonzola cheese! Then, I would wear my grungiest sneakers to this place barefoot. By the time I set my stench toes on the mats, the whole room would clear! The teacher would ask *Stinky Feet Ned* never to come back, and my parents would be too mortified to send me to a karate school ever again.

What can I say? What I'm missing in muscle, coordination, and dexterity, I make up for in brain power.

CHAPTER THREE

I'm proud to say I walked through the doorway to doom on my own two feet—right before Sensei Melissa told me to walk back out. Okay, so if I wasn't even walking right, it was going to be a long hour.

"Ned, whenever we enter or leave the dojo, we bow. Like this...." Sensei Melissa made two fists, stepped through the doorway, then bent forward at the waist.

I copied her, and my glasses slid an inch down my nose. I pushed them back up as Sensei Melissa simply smiled again.

But I bet I know what she was thinking: "Well, *my* job just got fifty times harder."

My tour of the mat room began with Sensei Melissa pointing to a wall. "So we bowed in toward this wall with the framed photograph," she said. "Any idea why?"

The man in the photo stood hands on hips, gray-haired. He wasn't angry, wasn't smiling. He just ... was.

No, enlighten me, I thought. To the teacher, I said, "No, Sensei Melissa."

"Every dojo has a family tree. Ours begins with this man, my father, who taught me karate. If a student of mine opens a school one day, he or she will hang up a photograph of my dad and of me. And so on. Who knows? If you stick with karate and train hard, maybe *you* will open a school one day."

Train hard? There's a better chance of me being hit by a train real hard.

"What's your father's name?" I asked to sound interested.

"We call him *Tora Khan*, which means Tiger King. Pretty cool, huh? Cool enough to name the school after him, anyway."

Before realizing it, I let out a low whistle. *Tora Khan.* Tiger King. Tora Khan. He sounded like a real-life superhero. What an awesome addition to the world of superhero crime fighting! Superman, Spider-Man, Batman, Iron Man ... Tora Khan! Wait ... he could be a video game character. *Tora Khan versus the Dojo Devil!* And with each cheat code, Tora Khan earns a new super-crazy karate move! And if you find the ultimate cheat code, his daughter, Sensei Melissa, suddenly appears and fights beside him!

"Way cool," I said and meant it.

"So, this is our *dojo*," she held her hands out, pivoting left and right. "The word means karate school in Japanese. You'll pick up most of the rules of a dojo by following the other students, or *karate-kas*. For now, I'll tell you this: We don't eat in here, drink in here, or wear shoes in here. And ... we don't touch the walls. Ask me why."

"Okay ... why can't we touch the walls?"

"Well, Ned. It's just a rule. In life, sometimes we have to follow a rule simply because of that—because it is a rule."

Sensei Melissa continued walking and pointed to a bunch

NED THE NINJA: RELUCTANT HERO

of strange objects hanging on the opposite wall.

"Umm ..." I gulped. "Is this what you use on the kids who screw up in class?"

She laughed. Not an evil scientist sort of laugh, but it wasn't a "happy, happy, joy, joy" laugh, either. Instead, she explained, "This is our Wall of Weapons," as if introducing me to her favorite uncle.

"But you have a sign on the other wall that says, 'karate means empty hands.' Anyone carrying one of those has their hands full of something!"

Sensei Melissa laughed again, then pursed her lips. "Do you want the kid explanation for that or the adult one?"

"Well, you have a sign in the corner over there that says, 'All start at the bottom.' So I'll take the kid version on my first day, thank you," I replied, not sure if I sounded wise or like the doormat I am.

"Fine. It means you are capable of fighting with nothing in your hands, even though weaponry is a part of our art. There's a bigger, better meaning to the term, though. But I can appreciate your desire to take one step at a time. We'll save the true meaning for another day."

Another day. She thought I was coming back here! Even if I did, the joke was on her: My own empty hands have dropped fine china, gotten caught on curtains, knocked people upside the head by accident, and can't manage opening the lid of a jelly jar half the time. If she wanted to put weapons in these hands one day, she was going to have to upgrade the insurance policy on this place big time.

Sensei Melissa must have noticed I wasn't too happy; she took down two sticks connected with a short piece of rope and said, "Don't worry, Ned. These are foam. Can't hurt you."

Lady, I can find a way to hurt myself on a marshmallow.

"These are called nunchucks." She tucked one stick under her arm and held onto the other. Suddenly the one under her arm came flying out at me.

I ducked.

Again she laughed, and I noticed the stick was once again tucked under her arm. "Nice ducking, Ned. But next time, don't put your head down. Always maintain eye contact with your opponent."

What I wanted to tell her was that I had made a science out of duck and cover, so I'd stick to my methods. After all, I was still alive, wasn't I? Instead, while pushing my glasses back in place, I asked, "How'd you do that?"

"Ancient karate secret!" she smiled. Then, "It's not as hard as it looks. You'll get the hang of it one day."

Yeah, like in another life.

"You won't be trying these out for a long time, anyway."

True. 'In another life' probably *was* a long way off. Unless, of course, I hung around here too long.

"Wait," I gulped as my eyes fell on something that was wrong on so many levels. "Whaaaa ... whaa ... whaa ... what are those?" I pointed to a set of mini pitchforks that looked like they could do some serious damage.

"Those are *sais*."

"What do you use them for?"

"Now? Or originally?"

"Umm...?"

She waved her arm at the Wall of Weapons. "Most of these weapons were originally farming tools that people came to

21

use for defending themselves because they had nothing else. Those chucks I showed you were for flailing wheat. The sais would till, or dig, the soil. And, those things over there? They are *tonfas*, and they would grind rice.

I simply stared and said nothing. Did my mother realize she was throwing me into an activity that involved weapons? I was nine years old before she let me use a dinner knife by myself. Surely these pitchfork sai things would be a deal breaker?

"So are you ready to line up for class, Ned?

"Umm ... I suppose so." Did I have a choice?

"Great. Oh, by the way ... these days, the sais are used to stab and gut an opponent."

CHAPTER FOUR

" Pick a dot," Sensei Melissa called as twelve kids joined us in the dojo. Guess that made me lucky number thirteen.

Bright red and white dots spotted the mats in rows. Red? White? Did it matter? I chose a white dot since the red ones reminded me of the blood I was sure to loose before the end of class. I mean how often did those sais on the wall wind up stabbing and gutting? I wonder if Mom asked if this place kept a full box of first aid supplies. No doubt my *old* Mom would have made sure of that. This new 'toughen up the boy' Mom probably asked Sensei Melissa to withhold band-aids if I should need them. She probably said, "He'll live."

So there I stood on my white dot, feeling like a dork in my sweat suit, but minding my own business, when I heard, "Grrrrrrrr!" behind me. The beast turned out to be a blonde kid with a very serious look in his eyes.

"Umm, what?" I asked.

"Grrrrrr!" he growled louder, and I glanced at his belt. Blue. I supposed that meant he could kick my butt from here to Japan.

I shrugged helplessly. In class two minutes and I got growled at. At least Beck mastered English somewhere along the line. When *he* tells me he's going to wipe the floor with me, he gets straight to the point.

"Ned," called Sensei, "We line up in rank order, so you're in Julian's spot. I need you to move down five dots. Thanks."

"Sorry, pal," I nodded at Julian, who grunted what I could've sworn was, "No problem, man." But in case he actually said, "I'll kick your can," I moved down to the fifth dot quickly. Red dot. Of course.

This move put me next to the tiniest girl I'd ever seen with the most orange hair I'd ever seen. I tried to be friendly:

"So I just stand here like this?"

"Unless you'd rather stand on your head," she giggled in a friendly way. Unfortunately, her giggling had me thinking she was cute, which had me turning red in the face. So by the time she asked me, "Is this your first class?" I couldn't speak any better than Julian.

"*Aswate!*" boomed Sensei's voice. The girl suddenly dropped to the floor on her knees. So did everyone else, which left me the only kid standing up.

"Hey, white belt! You have to kneel," said a voice at the far end of my row.

I dropped to my knees—hard. Apparently, the road to knee replacement surgery began here.

"Excuse me, Mr. Spencer!" Sensei Melissa's voice and expression suddenly changed—sort of like in those creepy movies when the nice hitchhiker you've just picked up wants your car, your money, and perhaps your life. "Do we call out in class?"

"No, Sensei. Sorry," said the boy with the green belt. His expression was as black as his hair, but for some reason he didn't seem threatening—just moody.

"Give me twenty push-ups while the rest of the class bows in."

"Yes, Sensei."

"Ned. Aswate is our school's word for 'kneel.' Keep an eye on Adrianna. She might be an orange belt, but she knows her stuff."

The tiny girl with the matching hair and belt smiled at me.

"Yes, Sir ... M'am ... Sensei," I said, wondering how insane butterflies had found their way into my stomach.

Sensei raised two fists and the class followed. "Ray!"

Quickly, I looked around for Ray again, but the whole class suddenly had their foreheads very close to the floor. I followed.

"*Rei* means 'bow!'" whispered Adrianna.

Again?

"Stand like a black belt," came the next command.

The class leaped back to standing as if they all operated at the press of one button. I followed, my knees complaining and my forehead throbbing. Yes, that's right: I whacked my head on the floor when I bowed. Go ahead and laugh. I'm used to it. I'll wait.

Sensei opened a book, pencil in hand. "Greg Spencer."

"Here, Sensei!" The green belt who yelled at me earlier breathed heavily as he did his last pushup. "Weren't my push-ups awesome? Did you ever see anyone do them so fast? Did you ever—"

"Clara Wheaton."

"Here, Sensei!" said a thin girl with a shy, squeaky voice. She was ghostly pale with a long brown pony tail and dark eyes. At first glance, I wouldn't believe she could kick over a blade of grass. Yet she wore a purple belt and stood further up in line; that had to count for something. Interesting.

Sensei went on calling names as I noticed Greg Spencer staring at me, probably taking note of who caused him to do twenty push-ups. My heart skipped a beat ... then another ... then another. Just as the rhythm got back to normal, I looked away ... straight into Adrianna's blue eyes, which caused my heart to stop again. Someone get me out of here!

"Peter Austin."

"Here, Sensei!"

"Julian Cobb."

"Grrrrrrr"

"Adrianna Ronan."

"Here, Sensei!" said Adrianna. Then she giggled in such a way that the dozen butterflies in my stomach mutated into full-blown flying saucers.

"Ned Herts."

"Umm ... here, Sensei?

"*Karate-kas,* this is Ned's first karate class. Luckily, he has joined a great group where he can expect your help and understanding as he learns the ropes.

Uh-huh. Ask my gym teacher how well I learn anything having to do with ropes. I ran my thumbs over my scraped palms.

"Ned, being a white belt means you know nothing and that it's okay to make mistakes. At this point, you can't get in

28

trouble for breaking rules. The colors of your belt will get darker as you gain knowledge, and you'll learn karate's rules by breaking them—but ... by breaking them only once!

I gulped.

"What's the matter, Herts?" Sensei Melissa laughed. "You suddenly went pale. Listen, part of the reason we mix ranks in classes is so the lower ranks can observe the higher ranks. And I fully expect those higher ranks to demonstrate following the rules. Right, Mr. Spencer?"

"Yes, Sensei! You can count on me to show how to follow rules more than anyone, because—"

"Ned, if you look around, you will see that Peter Austin and Clara Wheaton are the highest ranks in this class. They have been with me quite a while, and because of their excellent examples of teamwork, technique, and proper behavior, this class is full of karate-kas I am proud to have at my dojo." She paused, then looked me straight in the eye. "This is a safe place, Ned ..."

I glanced doubtfully at the sword on the wall behind her head.

"... where we respect each other. Bullying—whether physical or verbal—is forbidden here, and it has never been a problem in my dojo."

Ugh! What did my parents tell her?

"And class ... I know you will do your best to help Ned feel at home."

I heard, "Yes, Sensei" echo through the room, and then, "Grrrrrrr."

"Good! Now let's warm up!"

CHAPTER FIVE

I hate jumping jacks. Of course, when I do them they're more like "jumping jills." Clearly, I had bypassed the coordination room at the factory. I wouldn't mind so much if I had gotten an Einstein-level IQ or the sort of looks that cause girls whiplash as a trade off. Then again, it didn't seem like anyone had their best jumping jacks on display; Sensei suddenly shook her head and bellowed, "Ugh!"

We stopped, and a blue belt asked, "What's wrong, Sensei? You look sad."

"Sad?" said Sensei. "Mr. Dorchester, those jumping jacks were sad. You sounded like a herd of elephants!"

"Herd of elephants? Yeah, I've heard of elephants, Sensei."

Snort, snort.

I blinked. This blue belt—Dorchester—didn't sound like he was trying to be a smart alec; he actually thought he was funny and that the class would benefit from his sense of humor. Turns out I'm not the only dork in class! Fortunately, I do know when to keep my mouth shut.

"Ten push-ups, James Dorchester."

"Yes, Sensei!" said Dorchester way too eagerly and hit the floor.

"Guys, what's with the huffing and puffing? What's with the heavy feet? Martial artists are supposed to be silent and deadly. Your opponent would hear you coming from a mile away!"

"Sorry, Sensei," said Greg Spencer. "Should we do twenty push-ups for that?"

"Ggggrrrrr!" rumbled Julian.

"No, Mr. Spencer. That won't be necessary. Let's do

32

another set of twenty jumping jacks. Light on your feet, even breathing, please. Ready?"

Sensei turned in my direction and said, "Hi, Jimmy!"

I waved at her and said, "Umm ... I'm Ned, Sensei."

"What?" Sensei shook her head as if disoriented.

"My name is Ned ... not Jimmy." I pointed at James Dorchester. "I'm thinking he's Jimmy?"

The entire class busted out laughing. Dorchester actually rolled on the floor, and Julian roared like a choking hyena.

Sensei Melissa was trying not to laugh, but she lost it, too.

Adrianna was the only one who had sympathy on me. "No, Ned. *Hajime.* It's Japanese for 'begin.'"

"Oh."

Sensei choked out, "Hajime!" and we began.

Silent and deadly. Have to be silent and deadly. I'm the silent ninja. Silent and deadly.

My stomach rumbled. Uh-oh! Oh, no! But it was too late.

Just as we finished our twentieth jumping jack, Julian let out a low growl.

Adrianna snickered.

Peter, all the way at the end of the row, crinkled his face and moaned, "Ughhh!"

Greg grabbed his nose and whispered, "Man!"

It took Dorchester to state the obvious: "Sensei! Someone farted!"

My bright red face looked back at me from the mirrored wall across the room. I tried to make it go pale. I thought of the math test I had coming up. I thought of my mom's meatloaf. I thought about accidentally stepping on Jared Beck's foot.

Greg raised his hand, "Umm, Sensei?"

"Yes?"

Greg could hardly get the words out. "It seems that some of us are more silent and deadly than others."

Note to self: No more Mexican before karate class.

I don't want to sound like a wimp, but Sensei Melissa's warm-up routine almost killed me. Most of my push-ups began and ended on my face. My sit-ups made me wonder how I have enough strength in my back to stand up straight on a daily basis. And I did leg lifts in sheer terror of re-fried beans coming back to haunt me once more.

Then came stretching.

"Nice, Julian!" said Sensei. "Everyone look at how close Julian's nose is to his knee. That comes from practice."

Julian sounded like a purring motor, but I think he said, "Ain't I da' bomb!"

"Ned, reach for those toes!"

"Umm ... I am, Sensei," I eeked past the pain.

"Oh. Well, everything in good time, Ned."

Good time? Did someone say good time?

I caught a glimpse of my dad in the mirror. He held up both thumbs and flashed an encouraging smile. When Sensei wasn't looking, I stuck my tongue out at him. Instantly, Dad's face morphed into, "Now son, don't be a quitter!" mode.

I sighed. The dork doesn't fall far from the dork tree.

"Splits!" Sensei shouted so cheerfully that I wondered if she would sound the same shouting, "beating time!" or "root canal!"

So there I was, one leg in front of my body, one behind, and I was supposed to get close to the floor in that position. I began sliding down.

"Keep that knee straight, Ned!"

I moved lower to the floor.

"One hand on either side of your leg!"

Lower.

"Come on everyone. It's about flexibility."

Lower.

"Heads up!"

Lower ... uh-oh. Oh, no!

Adrianna, comfortable in a perfect split, leaned toward me. "Ned ... are you okay?"

I shook my head and stared at the seams in the blue mats, trying not to scream.

"Are you in pain?"

I nodded.

"Pull something?"

"Everything," I gritted between my teeth as panic set in. Surely my legs would never stand side by side again. How would I get back in the car?

"Well, if it hurts, come out of it." Sweet Adrianna. Get out of it? Who did I look like, Houdini?

"Can't!" I spat.

"Bend your back leg and lean to the side."

"Can't bend. Can't lean," I hissed.

"Umm ..." Adrianna looked over at Sensei.

"Wait," I gasped. "I've got it: Push me over."

"What?"

"Push me over sideways."

Adrianna shrugged, lifted one finger, poked my shoulder, and over I went. My legs, still split, hit Adrianna in the head on the way. Miraculously, she didn't yell, cry, or call me an idiot. Instead, she grabbed my forward leg and bent it at the knee.

I shrieked like an hysterical bird at a cat convention.

Sensei ran over. "Ned, what happened?"

Well, let's see. I just put my legs in a completely unnatural position, got stuck in front of the cutest girl I've ever seen, and had to ask her to rescue me. Oh, and then I kicked her.

"I ... I don't bend that way," I said.

"Seeing stars?" she asked.

"I think ... it's an entire solar system, actually."

Teaching a guy like me to kick is like teaching a gorilla ballet; he won't think to use it, and if he does, look out! And as far as my legs were concerned, asking them to kick after I treated them like pipe cleaners was just begging for trouble.

"Fighting stance!" came Sensei's command.

I glanced at the wall clock to discover I was only twenty minutes into my hour of torture. With a sigh, I tried to copy what everyone else was doing. One leg in front, knee bent ... *owww* ... fists up.

"I want to see correct technique in these front snap kicks, karate-kas. Ned ... you will see we lift the knee first, then kick with the ball of our foot. Do *not* use your toes."

And the ball of my foot is ... what?

"Ready? *Ichi!*" shouted Sensei.

The entire class kicked. I followed. Hey, not bad.

"*Ni!*"

We kicked again. *This* I could do!

"Higher! *San!*"

I kicked higher, and my back leg slid out from under me. Down I went.

No one made a sound, except for Julian, who I could swear said, "Tough break, man!"

I stared at the portrait on the wall—straight into the face of Tora Khan. Hey there, Tiger King. Meet the Spaz King. I am ... Spazo Khant. Capable of embarrassing himself in front of pretty redheads. Faster than a dead slug! Able to leap out of his skin at the first sign of Beck the Bonebreaker. Master of—

"Come on, Ned. My father, the Tiger King, always said karate is about getting back on your feet so you can learn to stay on your feet."

I wondered what Tora Khan would say when I wound up on my back in traction. Good riddance?

CHAPTER SIX

"So ... Sensei Melissa said you show promise, Ned. How about that?" said Mom from the front seat of our minivan.

I played with my seat belt and stared out the window. I would have stuck my tongue out at her, but Dad's eyes kept darting to the rear-view mirror for my reaction.

"Son? Your mother wants to know what you think about that."

I sighed. "You're the Board Game King. Don't you know a

'get out of jail free card' when you hear it, Dad?"

Dad's brow crinkled in the mirror. "What does Monopoly have to do with karate?"

I sighed again. "The sensei said I show promise so that she didn't have to feel uncomfortable telling you the truth. Sure, I show promise. Anybody shows promise. But promise for what? Promise to walk a straight line some day? Promise to walk out of that place years from now without tearing muscles to shreds? Promise to become Sensei's first major injury at her dojo? Do you honestly think she would say, 'Well, Mr. and Mrs. Herts, I'm afraid your son is the most uncoordinated lutz I've ever met. Perhaps you should just quit while you're ahead and have him take up knitting?'"

Mom grunted. "Ned, do you have to be such a downer?"

I didn't answer.

"Well, you *are* going to give it another go, aren't you?" Dad used his cheery voice.

"Dad, me doing karate is like an artist trying to draw without any hands."

Dad smirked into the rear view mirror. "Have you heard of

42

the MFPA, Ned?"

"The what?"

"The *Mouth and Foot Painting Artists Association*. It's for artists who use their mouths or feet to paint because they can't use their hands."

Through a snort, I said, "You made that up!"

"I most certainly did not. Look it up, kid."

I rolled my eyes. "It figures you would know about an organization like that."

"'Scuse me?" said Dad.

"Okay, how about this: Me doing karate is like a university professor teaching with half a brain."

Dad's face went smug. "While it's rare, there are people born with half a brain or who have one hemisphere removed because of disease. Many times doctors find—especially in people born that way—the existing hemisphere will take on the functions of the missing one. There are people out there who do just fine on half a brain."

I crossed my arms over my chest and pouted. "So, you're saying I'm doomed to be a complete know-it-all like you."

Dad smiled. "Well, I'd like to hope so. But no, that's not what I'm saying."

"Lay it on me, Dad."

"I'm saying that giving up on karate so soon just because you don't have much coordination sounds pretty wimpy when you've heard of accomplished artists who don't have use of their hands and people who function with only half a brain. Argue with that one, my boy."

I lay in bed that night wondering what to do about karate. Should I try one more class? On one hand, my legs still felt like they were in mid-split, reminding me of all the goof-ups that happened in just one class. I mean would you go back to a place where you kicked a pretty girl in the head after asking her to help you untangle your legs? To a place where you fell on your butt too many times to count, stunk up the entire room, and ran into a wall? What wall? Guess I didn't mention

44

that part. Let's have you, me, and the entire right side of my body keep it that way.

But how could I turn away from learning how to protect myself? I could hear Beck the Bonebreaker's constant threats running through my mind: "Hey, it's Ned the Nerd! Hey, Ned ... what are you doing after school today? Because I've got plans for you." Then there was his favorite line after inflicting physical harm: "Does it hurts, Herts?" And for some odd reason, the threat that always freaked me out most was, "Don't plan on entering any beauty contests for the next few months!"

But fear of Beck wasn't the only reason I thought I might try one more lesson. I could still hear Adrianna's voice right after class ended. She said, "I hope you join our class, Ned." I mean, you don't hope out loud that someone who kicked you in the head joins your class unless you really hope he does. Right?

Then there was the whole Tora Khan deal. He seemed beyond cool. Although, I have a feeling if Tora Khan actually walked into Sensei Melissa's school and saw she had allowed an uncoordinated lug to make a mockery of her dojo, he'd probably make her a white belt all over again. Was that something she might worry about?

But—and this is a very big but—if I could learn to look as cool as Tora Khan one day, I wouldn't be afraid of anything. And if I *was* afraid, I could beat that fear. I could walk straight up to Beck the Bonebreaker, flip him over my shoulder, look down into his terrified eyes and tell him how much lunch money he owed me—with interest!

If I did go back to that dojo, I could ask Sensei Melissa about all the things her father could do. It would be research, really, for creating the most awesome comic book. I mean, did Tora Khan leap through doorways, simultaneously taking out the biggest guy in the room? Could he fight thirteen people at the same time? Could he ... would he ... maybe he had some secret kick that ... *(yawn)* ... or a secret punch ... or a .....

I jumped. My eyes flew open. The window had rattled. Trees swayed on the other side of it. *Whew.* Just the wind.

I rolled over, my back to the window, and stared at the

classic *Star Wars* poster on my wall. Man, lucky Luke
Skywalker: He had Yoda. Then again, Luke had talent *and* the
Force. He just needed someone to teach him how to use it.
What did I have? Ooooh ... an A+ average in math. One day
that will make me a real hero to some remedial math student.
Ned Herts—Super Tutor. Yippee. On top of it, I bet somebody
would make me wear a cape.

The floor creaked behind me. I snapped around to see a
figure in black standing right next to the bed. With the sound
a glue-trapped mouse makes, I bolted upright and
immediately fell backwards off the side of my bed, sheets and
all. A scream wedged in my throat like a giant gumball while I
scrambled under the bed. Promptly, my head hit the wood
planks that hold up the mattress. I would like to say I blacked
out, but Murphy's Law wasn't through with me yet.

A pair of black boots came into view beneath the opposite
side of the bed. I gathered myself to shout for Dad, then
realized how dumb that was: My Dad is as physical as I am. If
he were to run into my room he could get himself killed! I
wasn't too happy with the guy at the moment, but I didn't

want him dead.

No, this was up to me. What did I learn today? Kicks? Splits? The power of a serious fart? With the instinct of a skunk in mortal danger, fear made the choice for me: One of my silent and deadly attacks erupted before I could take control over the matter.

A voice, deadly calm, said, "I'm looking for Ned the Ninja."

Oh, the wave of relief that washed over me! I shimmied backward and crawled out from under the bed. Before standing, I managed to say, "You've got the wrong house. I'm Ned the Nerd."

The voice chuckled, I think. I pulled myself together and stood, leaving the bed between me and ... and....

A wave of familiarity slammed my stomach into my tonsils. The man wasn't tall, yet his presence was huge! Gray hair, calm eyes of steel, dressed in black, he stood there as if he could demand the world's attention, and the world would respond, "Yes, what is it, Tiger King?"

Our eyes met. A yelp caught in my throat, strangling me worse than my mother's so-called surprise meatloaf.

Tora Khan's mouth curled as if he were about to snarl. We both stood frozen in silence when the great warrior suddenly grabbed his nose and said, "Ugh. What died in here?"

CHAPTER SEVEN

I don't know where it came from, but a rolled-up mat suddenly dropped onto my bed with a slap. Tora Khan unrolled it with one sweep of his hand, revealing an arsenal of weapons that made my skin crawl like a baby.

"Choose," said Tora Khan.

I hiccuped. "Live."

"What?" snapped the man in black.

"You're asking me if I want to live or die, right? I choose to live." I backed up a couple of feet, every cell vibrating in fear.

My head hit a shelf, sending fifty action figures diving for cover.

Tora Khan's lips moved silently, searching for patience. Then, "Choose *a weapon*," he said.

"Are you challenging me to a duel?" my voice cracked. "Because if you are, that's really unfair. I've had one karate lesson, and you should know that I didn't do very well. The best kick I did was completely by accident."

I thought of poor Adrianna for the hundredth time that night. Would I ever see her again? I had it all wrong; Tora Khan wouldn't make Sensei Melissa a white belt for letting me into her dojo. He would get rid of me himself. Maybe ... yikes, maybe Sensei Melissa actually sent him here?

"Wait a minute." Something suddenly occurred to me. "I didn't realize you were still alive."

As if he hadn't heard a word, Tora Khan repeated, "Choose a weapon."

I stared at the mat lying across my dinosaur bedspread. There were star-shaped discs with sharp edges, knives, a short sword, and three of those three-pronged things—sais—

that I had seen at the dojo. A set of nunchucks sat beside them. The rice-grinder thingie—a tonfa, Sensei Melissa had called it—there were two of them.

Suddenly, I saw my weapon sitting between two of the bladed stars. I picked it up and semi-confidently stated, "I choose this one."

Tora Khan stared. He plucked it from my fingers. "A toothpick? How did that get there?"

"It's not a weapon?" My heart sank.

"No, it's what I use on my teeth after eating salad." He flicked the toothpick to the floor. "Besides, what were you planning on defending yourself from with that? A fly?"

I gulped. Well, I had to start somewhere, didn't I?

"Choose."

I pointed to the nunchucks. At least they weren't pointy.

Tora Khan looked back and forth from me to the chucks. "No. Choose something else."

"You think I'll knock myself out with those, don't you?" I sighed. "Yeah, you're probably right. Umm ... how about this?" I picked up a four-pointed star, the outline of a tiger etched in red at its center. The edges of the points looked frighteningly sharp, but the object itself was small and possibly manageable.

"Are you sure?" Tora Khan asked in a way that made me realize he didn't know my self-esteem was already about as low as it could go.

"No, Sir. Of course not. I'm never sure about anything. It's probably best you understand that right off the bat ... or nunchuck, rather."

"Fine," Tora Khan muttered. Rolling his eyes, he removed the star and rolled up the mat, again with one sweep of his hand.

"Change." He tossed a small black stack of folded clothes onto my bed.

I cleared my throat. "Actually, I'm quite comfortable, really."

"We do not defend ourselves in Spider-Man pajamas," Tora Khan said.

"Oh. Too laid back, huh?"

"No ... Spider-Man is a sissy. Change."

I picked up the black clothes, practically in a daze. Spider-Man, a sissy? Oh, no, no, and no. Impossible. You don't mess with my hero.

"Take it back," I whispered.

Tora Khan narrowed his eyes, tilted his head. Did he not hear me or not understand?

I gathered myself. "I said, take back what you said about Spider-Man."

"Herts!" barked the Tiger King.

"Ye ... ye ... yes?"

"Let us operate in the real world for the moment, shall we?"

I nodded before obediently leaving my bedroom to change in the hallway bathroom. While I wrestled with the outfit, sorting out which flap of the jacket went where, I tried to wrap my head around the fact that what was happening to me was, according to the Tiger King, the real world. Clearly, I had drifted into one of those freaky realistic dreams. Tomorrow, I would wake up in the *real*, real world ready to face my mother's apple cinnamon oatmeal, a typical day of duck and cover, plus a math test. I shook my head; in the real world or the dream world, I never have control over anything. I returned to my bedroom for better or worse.

Tora Khan swallowed a sigh, then grabbed at the belt. "This is an *obi*, not a shoelace, Herts." He retied my belt, pulling both ends so hard that my breath whooshed out my mouth.

I couldn't take it anymore. I shut my eyes, held my breath, and reached out a finger. In what was probably the bravest move of my entire life, I touched his arm. It was solid.

Tora Khan ignored me, then pointed toward my bed where six strips of white cloth were on display. Each had a different red-and-black design along the middle.

"Choose," said Tora Khan.

There were Yin-Yang symbols, weapons, the image of a fist. But the design I picked up was an easy choice: a ferocious tiger jumping out of a yin yang. "This one."

Tora Khan came close to smiling. "Nice choice. The emblem of the Siberian Tiger."

"Does someone have that name, like how you are the Tiger

King?"

"My teacher," the man in black replied. He arranged the fabric strip around my head and pulled backward on the ends. I stumbled a few steps before he tied a knot at the back of my head with the clear intention of sending my brains oozing out my ears. I tried to wrinkle my forehead beneath the cloth. That wasn't happening.

"Ready?" Tora Khan asked.

"For...?"

"Herts. Are you ready?"

I was tired enough of unanswered questions to try sarcasm. "Yeah, you know me: I was born ready."

Tora Khan nodded, a satisfied smirk on his lips. "Follow me."

So I followed the mysterious man in black out of my room, down the stairs, and out my back door. He closed that door without a sound. He walked without a sound. And when he finally stopped, that bladed star shot out of his hand and slammed into a tree at the very back of my yard. *Thwack!*

"Get it," he said nodding toward the tree.

I froze. Maybe it was the cold night wind rushing into my nose. Or it could have been the icy dew of the grass on my bare feet. Maybe it was the sharp silhouette of Tora Khan's profile against the full moon, low in the sky. Whatever the cause, it suddenly hit me that if this was a dream, I wasn't waking up from it anytime soon. And, dream or reality, I was expected to take orders from a man who thought Spider-Man, truly a hero among heroes, was a sissy.

CHAPTER EIGHT

Six minor cuts on my fingers and a seriously sore arm didn't seem to matter to Tora Khan. And why should they? They weren't his fingers. Wasn't his arm! Clearly, a limb would literally have to fall off for the Tiger King to notice my pain.

"How many more times?" I whimpered, hopping from one foot to the other on the cold ground.

"As many times as it takes for you to stop throwing the star like a football."

The joke was on the man in black; I've never been able to throw a football properly. But I tried again, this time sending the star five feet away from the tree to ping against a rock. Once again, I ran to retrieve the star, feeling like a dog playing fetch. Out of breath, I stopped in front of the Tiger King and inspected the star for dents.

Tora Khan cleared his throat. He didn't look happy. And I knew I wasn't! The only happy thing in my backyard was the tree, because after an hour of being the star's target, it hadn't taken one hit. I began to imagine it dancing around, branches waving as if taunting, "Nah, nah, nah-nah-nah! You couldn't hit the side of a barn!"

"Focus on the tree," came Tora Khan's voice, measured and cold.

At that point, I lost it. "Oh, the *tree*! Focus on the tree? I'm sorry! I was aiming for the traffic light over on Demarest Avenue!"

Tora Khan's expression cut me down to size in an instant. I clammed up, set my eyes on the ground, then ordered myself not to cry.

"Again," came the command.

The moon had clouded over. The air was as cold as ever, and it chilled my sweaty skin. If my mother knew what I was doing, she would be babbling over me catching pneumonia, not getting enough sleep, etcetera, etcetera, etcetera.

I glanced up at my parents' window. All of this was their doing. I got my Dad's brainy genes and wimpy physique along with my mom's angelic conscience and meek manner. Maybe if it wasn't for my disastrous DNA recipe, I could put Beck in his place. I could tell Tora Khan that Spider-Man is *the* man, no matter what he thought. Better still? I could march myself up to my room this minute and go back to sleep.

My eyes drifted down the row of backyards, Jared Beck's far in the distance. I could just make out his trampoline, which had no net surrounding it. Near that was a marksman's board for his b.b. gun. I caught a glimpse of his tree house, which consisted of a platform with no walls. Did Beck's parents just not care, or were they raising him to grow up tough from day one?

I couldn't figure it out. Which was better? My hands-on,

active-parenting Mom and Dad, or Beck's laid-back folks? Wasn't there a happy medium for raising children? Some guide between dork training and bully training? And if so, why couldn't I have parents who knew about it?

I pulled back my heavy arm and snarled at the tree, deciding to blame it for everything I couldn't do. Then I let that star go. It spun, glinting in what was left of the moonlight.

Thwack! It struck the tree! Just barely, on the side, but it hit!

"Whooooeeeeee!" I shrieked, frosty breath shooting from my lips as I did a victory dance. I turned to Tora Khan with one hand raised in a high five.

The man in black left my hand hanging, walked to the tree, yanked the star out of the bark, then handed it to me. "Again," he said without the slightest hint of emotion.

"I'm sorry," I said, forgetting myself, "would you witness Luke Skywalker hitting his mark to blow up the Death Star and tell him to do it again? Would you shout, "Do-over!" to a firefighter who rescued a baby from a burning building?"

The guy just looked at me, unimpressed with my logic.

"You would, wouldn't you? Should've known."

Tora Khan gestured toward the forest at the edge of my lawn. "Again. Choose another tree."

I took the star and entered the woods, analyzing the trees one by one.

"Any tree will do."

I wheeled around to point out, "not necessarily."

"Herts. I haven't got all night."

"You might not know this, Sir Tiger King, but trees can't heal. When they have injuries, those areas no longer get food and water. So if a tree has enough wounds, it gets sick because food and water can't travel all the way up. Naturally, I'm looking for a tree that doesn't seem to have any injuries."

"Pick. A. Tree," the Tiger King growled.

I chose. I aimed. I fired. I missed.

Drizzle pattered onto my forehead.

"It's raining," I said.

"Will you melt?"

"Well, no ... but ... I could catch something."

A smirk sneaked onto Tora Khan's lips. "Herts, if you catch like you throw, you have nothing to worry about. Pick another tree, aim, and throw. We move quickly from now on."

Apparently, 'haven't got all night' is just a figure of speech, because it must have been around one-o'clock in the morning when I started flinging that star at tree after tree after tree. This little exercise seemed endless, and I began to wonder if the sun would climb above the trees before long.

But something happened by the middle of the forest. Instead of missing twenty times before hitting my target, it only took sixteen shots, then ten, then seven, then three. Then I made it through three trees without missing.

So I laughed. I shook my booty. I did the football dance players do when they get a strike. I ran around four trees like they were bases and shouted, "Gooooaaaaalllllll! Hey, Tiger King, did you see me slam dunk that thing into those targets? I think I got a triple!"

Tora Khan just stood there watching me. He didn't look pleased, but I didn't care. A guy like him is probably used to one victory after another. But not me! I was enjoying my moment in the sun ... um, moonlight. As I danced, the Tiger King walked behind me, probably to pull the star out of the last tree.

Hey. Who turned out the lights?

"Now try your throws going back to the house," said Tora Khan.

"But you pulled my blindfold over my eyes! What's that about?"

"*Hachikama* over your eyes!" corrected the Tiger King. He placed the star in my hand. "Hajime!"

Tears dripped down my throat. The frames of my glasses dug into my cheeks beneath the tight cloth. I hiccuped.

"Well, you're just ... mean!" I yelled. "What do you want from me? I've had one stinkin' karate lesson that I didn't even want to take, and you're acting like I'm Bruce Lee training for a competition. I've got news for you, pal: Bruce Lee would tell you where to go right about now. And ... and ... Spider-Man is *not* a sissy!"

I heard nothing in response, except for leaves shaking in

the breeze. The silence only made me madder. "Okay, so you've proven to me that if I were attacked by a bunch of trees, the trees would win. Anything else you would like to say to make me feel great about myself?"

"Concentrate, Ned. You came from this direction." Two hands turned me by the shoulders. "Focus. How many steps must you take before you are close enough to strike that last tree again? Was it a tall tree? Fat trunk? Short? Narrow?"

Wait.

I knew. Unbelievably, I knew! That last tree was narrower than most of the others. And I could probably get close enough with about five steps.

The wind surged and rain clouds finally let loose. Still, I raised my arm and threw the star, then held my breath until I heard a satisfying *thwack!*

"I got it, didn't I?"

"Actually, Herts ... that was my leg."

I screamed and almost pulled off my hachikama. Then....

"Joke, Herts. Yes, you hit the tree. Here..." Tora Khan placed the star in my grip again. "Continue. Where was the tree you hit before this one?"

I sucked my lips into my mouth and concentrated before walking twenty paces on a leftward angle. My foot tapped one of the roots I almost tripped over on the way in. The only difference now was that I expected the root to be there. Next, I caught the scent of a rotting log I had smelled just before the tree root. My next target stood right behind it.

With a smile, I stopped to wield my flying weapon. *Thwack!*

I turned left, walked two paces, then held out my hand for the star. Tora Khan was right there to place it in my hand. Carefully, I thumbed it around to get a good grip.

Thwack!

I grinned through the next five trees, knowing that aside from hitting bark, I was hitting on something about myself. Wasn't sure what that something was, but if nothing else, I would make a pretty successful blind guy.

There was no stopping me: *Thwack! Thwack! Thwack!* It seemed that even the rain clouds stopped flowing to watch me. Tree after tree, the star met bark with just one try. My heart pounded in triumph. Dream or not, this was the single-most, hugest achievement for me ever! Bopping to a made-up beat, I approached the last tree, spun around and let the star fly. *Thwack!*

Just when I realized we had reached the edge of my lawn, Tora Khan yanked the hachikama off my head. I blinked at the sky, which hinted at a rising sun. Raindrops dripped off the swing set. Muck mushed between my cold bare toes.

Speechless, I turned toward Tora Khan feeling like a completely different person. Unfortunately, you couldn't be speechless around Tora Khan for long; the silence would get real uncomfortable, real fast.

Finally, I said, "Not bad, eh?"

The Tiger King gazed at the lightening sky. "Sight is the strongest of the senses for most people. It's your weakest."

I threw up my hands. "What gave it away? My glasses? I mean, do you have any idea how to give a guy a compliment?"

"I just did."

I shook my head, "Huh?"

"You are ... unusual. Your sense of sight weakens the

success of your other senses. Sight throws you off. It brings you face to face with your many fears and uncertainties: fear of failure, bullies ... tree roots. Do you understand what this means, Herts?"

Give me algebra. Give me the basic principles behind fusion reactors. Heck, throw me a theory about why bullies like Beck exist, and I'll find a way to understand it. This mumbo jumbo about fear of failure? It flies over my head.

With a sigh, the Tiger King tried again. "When you hold onto your fears, they will come upon you fast, hard, and consistently. Fears limit us. Take away your fear by redirecting your thoughts about yourself and watch: Amazing things will start to happen for you."

I poked at the cuts on my fingers. "You know, I always thought that if Yoda was more straightforward with Luke Skywalker and didn't talk in riddles half the time, Luke wouldn't have had to deal with half the problems he did."

"Perhaps. But it would have made for a lousy film."

I looked up to debate the man in black, but two things occurred to me: One, he was gone. And two, for me, seeing could no longer be my requirement for believing. I think that's what Tora Khan tried to tell me.

Suddenly, in my head, I heard, "Get some sleep, Herts."

CHAPTER NINE

My radio alarm blared music at seven o'clock in the morning. There's nothing better than starting your day with a song about some unlucky sap losing the girl of his dreams yet again. The idea had Adrianna's face popping into my head. To erase it, I reached over to turn the volume down —and yelped in pain.

What was the deal with my shoulder? I closed my eyes, rolled onto my back and realized my shoulder wasn't the only problem. Sharp twitches attacked parts of my body for which science hadn't come up with names. And I was so tired! Believe it or not, I've felt better after beatings from Beck. Then again, Beck never made me do splits. How did one karate class make me feel this sore? And how was I going to get up, never mind get to school?

Today, school meant a huge math test. It meant mystery meat cheeseburgers on the cafeteria menu. It meant Mrs. Ginsberg's ultra-strong old lady perfume throughout history class. Oh, and it meant gym, where the rope climbing unit just might be the end of me. Did my body have the energy to tackle any of that today? Of course not. Did I have a choice? Certainly not. Need shower ... need wheelchair ... need ... sleep....

"Ned? Breakfast is ready. Hurry, or you'll be late." From the first floor, my mother's voice woke me a second time.

I grabbed my glasses off the night stand and threw them

on to pull the clock's fuzzy numbers into focus.

Uh-oh. Oh, no!

8:05.

My bus comes at 8:25.

No time to shower.

No way was I going to face mornings like this after every karate class. I had studying to do. I had comic books to read, superheroes to invent, and video games to play. Mom, Dad, and I were going to have a little talk today about their idea of raising a karate kid. I mean, in their *dreams!*

I froze, suddenly remembering something about a man in black, lots of trees, and cold feet. But I didn't have time to make sense of that crazy dream I had last night. It was stupid, anyway: Me, throwing Chinese stars? Me, training with the "Tiger King?" The truth was that any kid at Binghaven Elementary school would only expect me to hang out with the Nerd King—which, of course, explained why I spent a lot of time alone.

I swung my legs to the floor to find they were as useful as overstretched underwear elastic. Crippled-like, I hobbled to my dresser and grabbed clean clothes, which I threw over two layers of deodorant.

"Coming, Mom!" I shouted, running out of my room to make a wild grab for the stair rail. That's when I caught sight of my fingers, stretched out, reaching. That's when I dropped onto the top step, courtesy of my rubbery legs. I brought my shaking hands closer to my face. I counted: one, two, three, four, five, six, seven, eight, nine.

Nine cuts ran across four of my fingers, thin lines, crusted over brown.

"Ned?"

"Umm ... you know what? I'm really not hungry, Mom!" I called down the stairs before stumbling back to my room.

"But Ned! You have a math test today. You need a good breakfast."

What I needed was a good dose of hard, cold reality. You know ... reality ... that place where martial arts warriors don't appear out of nowhere to teach nerds how to throw deadly weapons. I yanked binoculars from a desk drawer and parted the curtains of the window that faced the backyard.

Eyepieces clattering against my glasses, I trained the binoculars onto the first tree I had aimed at in my dream.

"Ned," my mother walked into the room. No knocking in the Herts household! "Whatever are you doing? Looking for spies?" Then she laughed either at how cute she thought I was or how cute she thought she was being.

I froze again, binoculars resting on my nose. There it was: a slit in the bark. Although, that didn't officially make my dream real. All it did was make me more scared that I had lost my mind.

"Ned?"

"Yeah, Mom. Spies. That's it." I took a deep breath and shut my eyes. My dream came back to me: the whipping *thwacks* of the star hitting bark, wind and rain hitting my skin, hachikama tight around my head. Most of all, I remembered Tora Khan's voice, deep and commanding, saying, "Focus."

It was real—the whole thing. Yeah, I was still nuts, but that dream was no dream.

"By the way," Mom said, "did your father tell you he found

those *Karate Kid* movies from the '80s? Maybe you can watch one together tonight."

I shrugged, which caused my right shoulder to scream like a little girl. Now I knew why; I really had been throwing stars the whole night. Man, I hope Tora Khan offered a health insurance plan.

"Ned!" Mom leaned over between the wall and my bed. "How many times have I asked you?"

"Yeah, yeah, Mom. Karate movies. Fine."

"No, Ned." She stood up holding a small pile of black cloth. "How many times have I asked you not to leave your clothes on the floor? And ... why are they wet?"

As she began going into detail about mold and bacteria, I grabbed the pile.

"Sorry, Mom!"

"So why are they wet?"

Think fast, Herts!

"Umm ... I had an accident last night. Yeah. And I was too embarrassed to tell you. I'll take care of it! Bye!" I walked toward Mom, and she backed out of the room.

"But I don't remember you having black pajamas...."

I closed my bedroom door and locked it.

What was I to Tora Khan, anyway? An apprentice? An employee? Was he trying to be Batman and thought he could recruit me to be Robin? Did Sensei Melissa ask him to test me to see what I was really made of? Would he suddenly appear again? Did I want him to?

The clock caught my eye: 8:19 am.

I stuffed the damp black gi in my backpack and threw the strap onto my shoulder, biting back a howl of pain. Then, I ran—straight into my bedroom door, having forgotten I locked it.

Once out of my room and down the staircase, an alarming sight caught my eye: a muddy white towel on the floor of the downstairs bathroom. Making a quick detour, I swiped the hand towel and suddenly remembered wiping my mucky feet on it last night. I added it to the evidence in my backpack, beyond lucky Mom hadn't noticed it before I did.

Heading back toward the front door, I tripped over Cracker Jack, fell through the door, and tumbled down the porch steps. Cracker Jack barked several times as if I owed him an apology. As soon as my feet were under me again, the bus pulled up to its stop at the top of the block. Waving a hand, I stumbled over a newspaper, then floundered over four uneven squares of sidewalk. Fortunately, the bus driver saw me coming and held the doors open. He rolled his eyes as I threw myself onto his bus like a psychotic bat.

Tomorrow, I promised myself, I'd try all that with my eyes closed and see what happens.

CHAPTER TEN

Stomach rumbling, I lined up in the school yard and wondered how not having breakfast would affect my math grade. Bits and pieces from last night's escapade came popping into my head, too. Part of me still wanted to believe it was all a dream, but I knew better. My thoughts were finally returning to long division math problems when something pinged the back of my head. Before I could turn around, I felt it again ... and again.

A pistachio shell rolled past my foot. I sighed. This was

nothing new. I decided to ignore Beck, get the shells out of my hair later, and check my watch: One minute before the school doors would open.

"Ned!" Bobby Trayman hissed from behind me. "Beck the Bonebreaker is throwing pistachio shells in your hair."

"I know," I said without turning around. "Well, into everyone's hair a few pistachio shells must fall." And with that, a handful showered me, pooling down the neck of my shirt.

"Huh?" said Bobby. "Are you going to take that?"

Was he kidding? Of course I was. I always took everything Beck handed out.

"Well," I sighed. "It's not like it's silly string." And truly, I was thankful for that. Getting that stuff out of hair is a nightmare. We're talking at least three rounds of shampoo.

"Wuss," muttered Bobby.

I gulped. Was I really just happy that pistachio shells were not silly string? Bobby was right. I *was* a wuss. Tora Khan might have called me a sissy.

But I had nine cuts on my fingers to prove I wasn't wuss or

a sissy. I traced the scabs with my good fingers, then held both hands in front of me. These babies had actually thrown Chinese stars and thrown them well by the end of the night. And there was Beck—throwing pistachio shells. Now, I ask you: Who is the better ... the tougher man?

"Knock it off, Beck!" I shouted at the top of my lungs without turning around.

The playground went silent. Girls stopped talking. Boys comparing trading cards froze mid-trade. One first-grader's jaw dropped so far he could have licked his sneaker.

Heavy footsteps tromped from behind me. Slowly, I turned and met Beck's narrowed eyes. They were full of confidence, overflowing with fight, glowing with vengeance.

My head spun. My stomach slammed into my toes. I just screamed at Jared Beck. *What was I thinking?*

The first bell rang, and the school doors opened. Just as I took a step to follow the kid in front of me, Beck leaned in and whispered words that would haunt me all morning: "Ned the Nerd yelled at me? Well, today at recess Ned the Nerd is going to learn not to yell at me ever again." Then he turned and strutted to the back of the line, leaving me to walk to my classroom on the verge of hysteria.

My pencil shook as I took my math test. Knowing the answers was easy. Getting my hand to write them was another matter. The morning had gotten worse for me since Beck's threat; as soon as I sat at my desk, I realized my one real friend in the fifth grade, Tommy Douglas, was absent. That made the promise of recess even worse. At least Tommy *tried* to stand up for me from time to time. He had less of a chance of defending himself than I did, but Tommy was an all around good investment in a friend. Besides his loyalty, he was smart, could draw real well, and even stopped digging his nose this year. He would be a great partner for creating a new line of comic books some day. Of course, that would depend on me living through today.

In between math problems, I glanced through the window of my classroom door, across the hall, and into Beck's classroom. I could see the side of his thick head. The whole fifth grade was taking the same math test, and he was chewing his pencil.

It was obvious Beck was having a hard time with the test. No surprise there. I remember when he was in my class last year and never got higher than a 52 on any test. I'd take comfort in that, but beating Beck on a math test wasn't going to save me from his giant fists.

I wound up being the last kid to finish my test. That never happens.

"Are you feeling okay, Ned?" asked Mrs. Vilar from across the room. "You look pale."

"I'm okay," I lied. "Just didn't sleep well last night." Okay, so I half lied.

You might wonder why I didn't tell someone that Beck planned on making me his dessert after lunch. Well, I tried that in second grade and wound up in the principal's office *with* Beck while the principal threatened him right in front of me. I paid for that on the bus later that day ... the next morning and afternoon ... the day after that ... and the day after that. Adults: They think they're helping. If they only knew. Luckily, Beck isn't allowed on the school bus anymore. The reason? The bus schedule went into chaos every time the driver had to rescue one of the students from Beck. Let's play a game: Take a wild guess which student had to be rescued.

I ate lunch as far away from my nemesis as possible. Still, the cafeteria was typically safe enough. The lunch aides were all eyes, constantly on alert for a food fight. My theory is that they just didn't want to clean up the mess. It was a different story out on the playground.

Four aides occupied the school yard when I made a beeline out of the cafeteria. As always, they huddled together, chatting, gossiping, and sometimes sipping coffee. Some third grader could be hanging from a giant jungle gym bolt by his underwear, and they would be clueless to his suffering. There are days I still think I have a wedgie.

Normally, I hang out at recess with Tom, my M.I.A. buddy. Sometimes we talk movies. Sometimes we kick around a soccer ball. Sometimes a group of girls will recruit us to play house, school, the bad guys in some super-girl action adventure, or hold the ends of their jump ropes. We only did the jump rope thing once. Tommy has a bit of a crush on Mary Reese, so we agreed, but the laughter from every boy in the school just wasn't worth it, even for Tom.

Today, most of the girls huddled together in groups like future school aides, so I ran behind the kindergartner's jungle gym and around the edge of the building. I knew Beck would find me eventually; there was no doubt about that. The question was, how long could I hold him off?

I jumped into the fighting stance I learned in karate class and practiced my front snap kicks. After that, I squeezed my fists tight and threw some upper cut punches. The moves felt tough, like I was in control, but I didn't think they would help me against Beck.

With a leap that probably looked like a penguin attempting to fly, I turned around and tried my kicks again. This time I counted in Japanese as best as I could remember: *ichi, ni, san* ... umm ... *go*, stop, *hachi*, ro, froyo ... umm ... *cuatro, cinco, seis....*

I froze, shut my eyes. The sickening sweet smell of grape bubblegum flew up my nose. He was behind me, seething, and ready to teach me a lesson. With every cell in my body, I felt him standing there, ready to pounce. And he wasn't alone.

Without a word of warning, Beck leaped forward to wrestle me to the ground from behind. Only I knew it was going to happen, felt it deep in my bones. Without thinking, without turning around, I reached out one foot and took a simple, giant step to the left.

Beck fell right where I stood moments before, his nose level with the gritty cement. The crowd, half the recess population, let out a low, "Whoa!"

I just stood there as Beck slowly lifted his scraped-up face to turn on his side and stare at me.

I stared back—just for a moment, but in that moment, a weird feeling came over me. Not bad weird, *good* weird—as if I patted myself on the back for a job well done. I felt strong and ... aware of being strong. I felt as if that strength flowed from my eyes, wrestled the shock in Beck's eyes, and won the match. But that weird feeling wasn't simply strength. So what was it? I wouldn't find out that day, but I held onto the idea that there was something good about it ... something I wanted to feel again.

Like a slow-motion film, the shock on Beck's face melted into a dangerous sneer. A thin ribbon of blood ran from his nose onto his lips, which opened long enough to shout, "I *wanted* to do that, man!"

I took several steps backward and wondered if making it to Japan on a sprint was possible. Beck hauled his big body off the ground. He glanced around at the kids who seemed to expect an explanation from the fallen giant they either worshiped or feared. Wiping gritty hands on his jeans, he shouted, "You think I'd actually jump you like that on purpose, Herts? I'd get expelled! I just wanted to scare you,

Nerd! But when we're off school grounds? Look out: You're gonna hurts, Herts."

The crowd thinned as the Bonebreaker stomped back the way he came to nurse his wounds away from spectators. But if falling to the cement left Beck's spirit broken, it didn't stay that way; a quick bash of his shoulder against mine suggested I would, indeed, pay for my little victory at some point.

As the school aides finally looked up from their coffee to notice most of the kids had bunched around the bend, Julian from karate class stepped out from a group of sixth graders. He approached me with grins and growls. Being the hot-and-happening social butterfly I am, I had no idea he went to my school. So what if the aides were finally acting like they safeguarded the schoolyard by fussing over Beck and telling kids to go back to their activities; I had someone who could actually do karate standing next to me! The brief moment of security was all I needed to breathe properly again.

"Grrrrr rrrrrggg!" Julian said and offered me a handshake.

"Thanks!" I smiled. "It *was* a nice move. But I'll probably get suspended. Beck will say I pushed him or something."

Julian shook his head and laughed a growl that reminded me I didn't actually lay one hand on Beck. He also claimed that Beck would never admit someone else took him down.

"I hope you're right. Hey, do you think I should tell Sensei what happened?" I asked. My hand nearly slammed over my mouth; had I decided to go back to karate class? You know, I think that tiny moment when Beck was on the ground and I was standing tall, our roles briefly switched, might have made the choice for me.

Julian's grin turned sly. "Ggggggrrrrr...rrrr..ghruu...grr!"

"What do you mean, how else will Adrianna find out about it without me bragging?"

Julian growled something to the effect of, "Sensei will use it as an example of bushido to talk about with the class."

"What's bushido?"

Julian laughed and grunted, "Look it up!" Then he turned to go just as the bell rang, ending recess.

"Wait ... why would you think I want Adrianna to know?"

Julian pivoted back and said, almost clearly, "Because she's my neighbor, and if I have to hear, 'I hope Ned joins karate class,' one more time, I'm going to throw up!"

That night, I hit the Internet to look up *bushido* in a Japanese-English dictionary. It read, 'honor code of the Samurai: courage, loyalty, mastery of the martial arts, self-discipline, and wisdom.'

What was so bushido about me taking one step to the left? I might be a borderline genius, but I had to think a long time before I figured it out: Taking that step showed wisdom, because I chose the simplest path out of danger. And because it was the least aggressive path to dealing with Beck's attack, it showed self-discipline. Although, let's not kid ourselves: I would have froze into an ice sculpture before laying a hand on Beck.

Still, *bushido* was something *I* could have one day. But if I really wanted it, I *would* have to go to karate class. I would have to stop complaining about my shoulder, my legs, every ache and pain. I would have to welcome the mysterious Tora Khan with a smile on my face, instead of a knot in my throat. That is, if he ever shows up again.

Maybe Ned the Nerd *could* become Ned the Ninja. Maybe I'd ask Adrianna what she thought.

THE END

(... of the beginning)

ABOUT THE AUTHORS

Kea Alwang lives in New Jersey with her podcasting husband, film-obsessed son, book-munching daughter, and a self-absorbed parakeet. Apart from writing and world building, she teaches Isshin-ryu karate, searches for the perfect chocolate bar, and immerses herself in multiple fangirl obsessions.

Her other works include the Young Adult Speculative fiction series, *Based on a Dream*. Find Kea online at: www.keaalwang.com, www.basedonadreambooks.com, and www.infiniteinkauthors.com.

Melissa Mertz owns and operates *The Dojo Paramus* in Paramus, NJ, where, as a 5th level Black Belt in Isshin-ryu, she has taught for over ten years. She is forever grateful for the opportunity and privilege of teaching martial arts to those who have trained with her. She thanks her students and their parents for their trust and for following her path to Black Belt. Melissa lives in New Jersey with her star-throwing son and the sweetest dog the world over.

Made in the USA
Charleston, SC
03 May 2016